D1298919

STERLING CHILDREN'S BOOKS
New York

An Imprint of Sterling Publishing
387 Park Avenue South
New York, NY 10016

ISBN 978-1-4027-8435-4

Library of Congress Cataloging-in-Publication Data Available

Distributed in Canada by Sterling Publishing
c/o Canadian Manda Group, 165 Dufferin Street
Toronto, Ontario, Canada M6K 3H6
Distributed in the United Kingdom by GMC Distribution Services
Castle Place, 166 High Street, Lewes, East Sussex, England BN7 1XU
Distributed in Australia by Capricorn Link (Australia) Pty. Ltd.
P.O. Box 704, Windsor, NSW 2756, Australia

For information about custom editions, special sales, and premium and corporate
purchases, please contact Sterling Special Sales at 800-805-5489
or specialsales@sterlingpublishing.com.

Printed in China
Lot #:
2 4 6 8 10 9 7 5 3 1
07/12

www.sterlingpublishing.com/kids

SILVER PENNY STORIES

Puss in Boots

Told by Diane Namm
Illustrated by Denis Zilber

Once there lived a miller with three sons. The eldest son was the smartest. The middle son was the strongest. The youngest son was the handsomest lad in the village.

One day the miller announced, "It's time for me to retire. You must each make your own way in the world."

"You are the smartest," he told his eldest son. "I give you my mills."

"You are the strongest," the miller told his middle son. "So, to you I give my mules to care for."

"Thank you, Father," both sons said happily.

The miller turned to his youngest, favorite son.

"I have a very special gift for you, my boy," he said.

The miller handed his handsome son an enormous, wide-eyed cat.

"Thank you, Father," the handsome lad said, trying to hide his disappointment.

"This cat brings good fortune," the miller promised.

Then he sent his son away with a hug and the cat.

Before long, the cat turned to the handsome son.

"I'm going for a walk all day and I'll need your boots," he said.

The handsome son was too surprised to protest.

The cat slipped into the boots and stood up. "And I'm going to need that feathered hat," said the cat. "I'll be back soon!" he called.

Then he disappeared into the woods.

The handsome son settled down to wait for the cat to return.

Meanwhile, Puss in Boots, as he had named himself, set out to make the young man's fortune.

Puss in Boots caught a large fish.
He traveled to the king's palace
and presented it to the king.

"A gift from my master," Puss said
with a deep bow.

"Take me to meet the master of such an extraordinary cat," said the king.

"Follow me," Puss said with a smile.

He raced quickly ahead of the king's carriage, back to where he'd left his master.

"Hurry, Master," the cat said,
"Give me your clothes and jump in
the river."

"Why?" he asked, but he did what
Puss said.

"You'll soon see," answered the cat.

Puss hid the clothes deep in
the woods.

Then he waited by the side of
the road.

Soon the king's carriage arrived,
with the king and his beautiful
young daughter.

"Where is your master?" asked the king.

"A terrible thing has happened, Your Highness," Puss said. "Robbers have taken my master's clothes!"

"Where is your master now?" the king asked.

"He is hiding in the river," said Puss in Boots.

"We must help him at once," the king's daughter said.

The king handed Puss in Boots
a royal blanket.

The cat ran to the river.

"Master, put this around you. Come
with me!" he said.

The young man followed Puss to the carriage by the side of the road.

"Your Majesty, I present my master, the Duke of Flim-Flam," Puss said with a deep bow.

"Ride with us," said the king.

Astonished, the young man climbed into the carriage.

"Take him to our palace down the road, please," Puss said. "I will run on ahead."

Puss ran quickly down the road
to the palace of a terrible wizard.

"I bet you can't change yourself
into a mouse," Puss challenged.

"Of course I can!" boomed
the wizard.

And with a flash, he did.

Puss pounced on the wizard-mouse and ate him, just as the king's carriage arrived.

Puss greeted them with a deep bow.

"Welcome to the duke's palace," he said, and winked at his master.

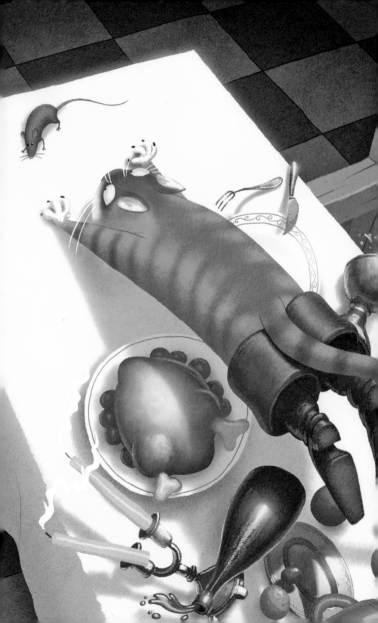

The king was impressed. He decided
at once that his daughter should
marry the duke.

The handsome young man, his
beautiful princess, and Puss in Boots
all lived happily—and royally—
ever after.